Natalie

Really Very Much Wants to Be a Star

Other titles in the That's Nat Series

Natalie and the One-of-a-Kind Wonderful Day!

Natalie Really Very Much Wants to Be a Star

Natalie: School's First Day of Me

Natalie and the Downside-Up Birthday

Natalie and the Bestest Friend Race

Natalie Wants a Puppy, That's What

Natalie

Really Very Much Wants to Be a Star

Dandi Daley Mackall

ZONDER**kidz**

ZONDERVAN.com/
AUTHORTRACKER
follow your favorite authors

We want to hear from you. Please send your comments about this book
to us in care of zreview@zondervan.com.

For Lawson ❖.

ZONDERKIDZ

Natalie Really Very Much Wants to Be a Star
Copyright © 2009 by Dandi Daley Mackall
Illustrations © 2009 by Lys Blakeslee

Requests for information should be addressed to:

Zonderkidz, *Grand Rapids, Michigan* 49530

Library of Congress Cataloging-in-Publication Data

Mackall, Dandi Daley.
  Natalie really very much wants to be a star / by Dandi Daley Mackall.
    p. cm. — (That's Nat!)
  Summary: When Natalie does not get the lead role in the Christmas play at her church,
she struggles with disappointment and jealousy until she experiences the true meaning of
the holiday.
  ISBN 978-0-310-71567-2 (softcover)
  [1. Theater — Fiction. 2. Christmas — Fiction. 3. Jealousy — Fiction. 4. Christian life — Fiction.
5. Sunday schools — Fiction.] I. Title.
  PZ7.M1905Nm 2010
  [Fic] — dc22   2008049738

Editor: Betsy Flikkema
Art direction and design: Merit Kathan

Printed in the United States of America

13 14 15 16 17 18 /DCI/ 20 19 18 17 16 15 14 13 12 11 10 9 8 7

Table of Contents

1. A Few of My Favoritest Things...............7

2. Sunday School...13

3. New News...21

4. Honest and for True!..........................30

5. Pilots and Herod...................................35

6. Castles!...41

7. Waiting a Hundred Gazillion Days ... 49

8. And the Answer Is ... .57

9. 'Hearsals...66

10. Costumes...72

11. Snowladies..79

12. Really Much Christmas! 86

Chapter 1

A Few of My Favoritest Things

When I'm all grown up, I am going to be a famous movie-star actress who goes by the name of Natalie 24.

And that is already my name.

Plus also, sometimes when my mommy and daddy are in a bad mood, I go by the name of "NATALIE ELIZABETH!"

And my other favorite names you should know are Percy, my very own cat. Which is also my mommy and daddy's cat. I love that cat Percy.

Plus too, I very much love all cats. Except for when they scratch me.

Percy also goes by the name Percy 24. Or sometimes Creature.

Like when he jumps up on our kitchen table that is in our kitchen. My mommy shouts, "Get off of that table, you Creature!"

She means Percy.

Usually.

Because sometimes when you're five and a half, you wonder things.

Like what that would feel like to climb up and sit on that kitchen table.

And what would it feel like to eat off of that kitchen-table chair when you are sitting on that table — instead of the other way around.

And if you do something about all that wondering, then all that shouting of "Get off of that table, you Creature!" might could be at you. And not your cat this time.

In case you are five and a half years old and you wonder like I wonder, I will tell you this. It doesn't feel that good to sit on a table and eat off the chair. On account of you have to lean way, way down to get your spaghetti off your plate.

And that slippery spaghetti stuff has enough trouble of its own making it into your mouth. That's what.

I love spaghetti really much.

Only I wish they made spaghetti purple. I love purple. On account of it is so purpley.

I love movie people. Beautiful movie people who act in movies. And I'm going to be one of those movie-acting people myself when I am grown up. Remember?

Nobody except Percy knows this secret going-to-be-a-movie-actress thing about me. And that is 'cause I forgot this secret thing my own self. And I only just started knowing it again last week.

I think I will be a singing movie-star actress. On account of I very much love songs.

I love that song about monkeys jumping on the bed. And I can sing some of the words to that song.

I love that church song about those guys who go by the name of Hark and Harold Angel. It goes, "Hark and Harold Angel sing! Glory to that newborn King!"

That song is one of Carol's songs. And she means Jesus by that newborn King part. And I very

much love Jesus. That's what.

Another of my favorite Carol's songs goes, "Jeremiah was a bullfrog. A really good friend of mine."

I just pretend-sing the next part 'cause the words are all squished together anyway. And it ends up, "Joy to the world! All the boys and girls! Joy to the fishes ..." and like that.

I love that song. And it has in it other things I love.

Frogs.

And bulls.

And good friends, which I have some of.

Like Laurie. And that is one more name you should know about. Plus also, one of my favoritest things.

Laurie is my bestest friend who is a girl.

Plus also, Jason. Jason is my bestest friend who is a boy. And that's not the same thing as a boyfriend.

Even though the friend who is a girl is the same

thing as a girlfriend. If you are a girl to start with.

And that can get your head mixed up if you think about it.

There's one more thing I love more than cats and purple and movie stars. And that is special days.

Like my birthday, which goes by the name of February 4.

And that other great day that I love for my most favorite day is Jesus' birthday. That's what!

And it goes by the name of Christmas.

Plus, it is coming!

Soon!

Chapter 2

Sunday School

We have very much hurrying in our house on Sundays. On account of we all go to sunny school and church. The real name for that school, which doesn't feel like a school, is Sunday school 'cause it happens on Sundays. But when I was too little to know that, I called it "Sunny" school. That was a silly name on account of we go there even when it isn't sunny a little bit outside.

Like today. We've got snow out there! And this is one more of the favorite things I love.

Plus also, Sunday school is a favorite thing I love. Except for that hurrying part.

"Hurry, Nat!" Daddy yells.

This can be a hard thing about yelling. There is a lot of that yelling going on at our house before Sunday school. But you can't do any of that yelling when you get there.

"Coming!" I yell back.

But I am not really coming.

This is still not a lie. I only need to look more into my closet for something. Then I will really be coming. And that something I got to find before

then is a purple dress.

I love my purple dress. I wear that thing every day to Sunday school. Because it's so purpley. That's what.

"Natalie Elizabeth!" Mommy yells. She yells this very loud. Which she would not need to do 'cause she is right here in my bedroom.

"Why aren't you dressed yet?" she still yells.

"I'm looking for that lost dress," I say. And this is a true thing.

"I set your dress out on your bed for you, Nat. All you have to do is put it on," Mommy says back.

This is a true thing, also. Only that dress on my bed isn't purple. It's green. Green is a boy color.

I look at that green dress. Then I look more in my closet. "Mommy, that dress isn't purple."

"Natalie, your grandmother gave you that dress last Christmas." Mommy picks up that dress and carries it to me and my closet and puts it over my head until my arms poke out.

"It isn't purple," I say again. Because maybe she forgot that part.

"It looks just fine, Nat," Mommy says. "You left your purple dress on the floor last week. It's in the wash. Besides, green is a Christmas color."

"Why?" I ask. "How come purple isn't a Christmas color?" I think this is a good idea to make purple a Christmas color. I think baby Jesus loves purple. Like me.

"Not now, Natalie," Mommy says. She says this in her aggravated voice. And *aggravated* is what other mommies call mad.

I have to pull at the top of that dress because the green is itchy.

Mommy holds my hand and walks out of my bedroom. My hand goes too. Plus also, the rest of green me.

Honk! Honk! Buddy yells.

Buddy is our car. And I'm the one who called it by that name. My daddy says Buddy is a good name for a car.

Honk! Honk! Buddy yells again.

Mommy puts on my flowery pinkish and purplish coat. Plus my woolly purple hat that will go over my face if I want it to. Plus my snowy boots. Plus my gloves.

It is really much hot in here.

Honk! Honk! Buddy yells.

Mommy says something very much soft. Then
she slips only one arm into her coat and opens our
door to outside.

The snow quit. There's not even enough snow
to make snowballs out here.

"Hurry, Nat! We'll be late!" Mommy yells.

Daddy drives very fast to Sunday school. I
know this because my mommy says so.

Mommy says, "Don't drive so fast."

17

Daddy says, "Would *you* like to drive?"

I think they are maybe aggravated at each other.

Once upon a time, when I was aggravated at my granny, I hollered, "You are not the boss of me!"

She hollered back, "Yes I am!"

"Hey!" I holler very much loud from the backseat.

They stop their loud talking.

"Who's the boss of our house?" I ask. I think this might could be a good thing to know.

Mommy's face stops looking aggravated. She gets big in her eyes. Her mouth turns smiley faced.

Daddy looks at my mommy, and his face turns smiley also. "Hmm," he says. "I'm the boss of our house, of course!" He winks at Mommy. "Because your mommy says so."

They are smiley faced at each other.

"True," Mommy says. "Your daddy is the boss of our house … until Granny comes over. Then he's just one of us."

They laugh their heads off.

Only I don't get it.

Mommy and Daddy are still laughing when they walk me to my Sunday school classroom.

"Natalie, be good in Sunday school," Mommy says, pulling off my hat and coat.

She leans down and kisses me on my eye.

But my eye sees it coming. So it's just the skin part that gets kissed.

"Okay," I say. And I mean this.

I like Sunday school.

"Don't talk too much, Nat," Daddy says. He peeks inside the door.

And that's my classroom in there.

I nod. Which is talking less than if I say okay.

Mommy and Daddy walk away. Together.

Without me.

I am just standing here looking at the backs of my mommy and my daddy.

Those backs get littler and littler.

Then they disappear.

I keep on standing here in the doorway.

I keep on looking at where my mommy and daddy were.

And aren't now.

I get chokey in my neck, like there's a rock in there. It's not a real rock. But it feels like a real rock that I swallowed. But it didn't go down.

I know my mommy and daddy are only just walking down the hall.

And then turning.

And then walking down another hall.

And then going into Big Church.

But it feels like they are walking more away than this.

Chapter 3

New News

My mommy and daddy are only just in Big Church.

I have been to Big Church sometimes. Big Church is not so much fun as Sunday school.

The only talking you get to do in there is singing. And you have to stand up to do it.

Plus also, your feet don't touch the floor when you sit down on those PUs. This is fun at first. Like you think it's going to be. You can swing your feet.

Then somebody will make you quit it. That's what.

So it's not so much fun for so long as you thought it would be.

You don't get to do anything in Big Church.

They don't color in there.

They don't answer questions from their teacher.

In Big Church, they don't even gotta pray. They got a guy who does it for you.

This makes Big Church take a whole lot longer than Sunday school.

"Nat! Come sit by me!" Laurie shouts.

I know this is Laurie because I can tell by how those words sound. Plus also, I can tell this without looking.

I turn around so I'm more in the classroom than I am not in the classroom.

Laurie waves at me.

Laurie is that bestest friend of mine who is a girl. She has yellow hair that curls all over the place. And it is doing that right now.

I wave back.

Plus, I run to sit in the special saved chair by Laurie.

The rock thing in my neck goes away.

"I like your dress," says my bestest friend, Laurie.

Laurie says this even though she sees this boy-green dress a very lot on me.

"Thank you," I say.

On account of Laurie saying that nice thing about this dress that isn't so much new. And isn't purple.

Laurie is like that.

I love Sunday school.

"Hi, Jason!" I yell to my friend who is a boy. But not my boyfriend. I have to yell this because he is three people away.

"Don't yell, Natalie," says Mrs. Palmer. But she says this while her mouth is still smiling and she is still a smiley face.

Mrs. Palmer is very good at doing this trick. She can stay smiley faced even when you're running around the room.

Or being chased.

Or chasing.

Mrs. Palmer can yell, "Natalie, please sit down!" And she can do that without un-smiling her mouth. I think this makes her a really much good teacher about God.

I very much like Mrs. Palmer.

I don't want to yell. So I get up from my seat.

"Save my seat, Laurie," I say. Just in case.

And here's why there's a just in case.

There is a girl in this Sunday school class. And she goes by the name of Sasha. And she is sometimes not very nice.

That's what.

Plus also, she will steal seats.

I have seen her do this my own self.

I walk over three chairs because this is where Jason is sitting. "Hi, Jason," I whisper. I feel good

about whispering this. Whispering is not yelling. And "Hi" is not talking too much.

"Would everyone please take your seat?" Mrs. Palmer yells.

I am the only one not already taking my seat.

"Now!" Mrs. Palmer yells.

I smile at her because her mouth is still smiling at me. And her face is still a smiley face.

"Mrs. Palmer, I think you're yelling," I tell our teacher. I say this because I know she doesn't like yelling. But maybe she forgot that part.

Or, she maybe doesn't know she's yelling.

People's ears get old when they are old all over.

And Mrs. Palmer is as much old as my granny.

Those old ears make it hard to hear.

I know this because it happened to my own granny. That's what.

Old ears make your mouth yell because you can't hear your own talking.

So Mrs. Palmer's old ears are probably like that. She probably doesn't even know she is yelling. Which is why I tell her so.

I like her that much.

"Sit down, please, Natalie," Mrs. Palmer says too loud.

Poor old Mrs. Palmer.

Laurie did a very good job saving my seat.

I sit in it.

"All right, class," Mrs. Palmer yells. "I have some news for you!"

I do not care that she is yelling this. I LOVE news for you!

Except for when my mommy is aggravated.

And she says, "Well, I've got news for you, missy."

"Be really quiet, children," Mrs. Palmer yells. "Because I have an announcement!"

I LOVE 'nouncements! 'Nouncements are when you know something other people don't. And you tell them. And they say "Ah!" or "Wow!"

'Nouncements could be telling you that you are going to Disneyland. Like, "I have a 'nouncement! We will all be going to Disneyland for Sunday school."

Or, it can be other stuff. Like, "I have a 'nouncement. This year, Christmas will not take so long to get here. And there will be more presents!"

But it is always *new* news.

I love new news.

Our room sounds like bumbly bees got loose in here. That's how excited we are about this new news.

"What is it, Mrs. Palmer?" Sasha asks. She has on a purple dress. I would very much like that dress if Sasha didn't have it on.

Plus also, she has purple shoes.

And purple socks.

And a purple bow.

"Well, I need to have everybody quiet as a mouse before I can make my announcement," Mrs. Palmer says while she's still smiley faced.

Sasha turns in her chair and frowns at us. Her chair is always the one on the front of our room. In the middle.

And sometimes she steals that chair.

Sasha puts one of her fingers over her mouth and says, "*Shh-h-h-h!*" She sounds like an aggravated snake.

Sasha can't say *Shh* and smile at the same time.

She is *not* our teacher.

We get all quiet.

Not because of Sasha.

"All right, class. Are you ready for this?" Mrs. Palmer is showing all of her teeth. Plus a whole lot of the skin part that grows above her teeth.

And that's how I know this is going to be the

very bestest new news I have ever heard in my
whole life.

"This year," Mrs. Palmer says, smiley facing all
around the room, "our Sunday school class is going
to put on a Christmas play for the whole church to
see!"

Chapter 4

Honest and for True!

A Christmas play! I can't hardly believe my young ears.

"Honest and for true?" I ask.

I know Mrs. Palmer is a truth-teller of Bible things. Only some of the times, even truth-teller grown-ups tease stuff to little kids. And you can't be too careful.

Mrs. Palmer smiley faces at me. "Honest and for true. This class will act out the play for our Christmas Eve service."

We are going to be the movie-star actors in that Christmas play! That's what!

I always knew I'd be a famous movie-star actor when I grew up. Only I'm not even grown up.

"Wow! Wowee! Wow!" I yell.

I am not the only one yelling this. I only yell it more louder.

Mrs. Palmer covers up her old ears with her hands. That's how loud I am yelling.

"Children, please," Mrs. Palmer says. "Let's settle down so I can tell you more about it."

"When can we — ?" I start asking.

Mrs. Palmer stops me asking. "Wait. Why don't you just hold up your hand if you have questions, okay?"

"Okay!" I yell.

Then I hold up my hand very high. I wave that hand like crazy. My other hand has to help out holding so I can wave it louder.

My hand is waving so hard that it's pulling me right out of my saved seat. That's what.

Plus also, all that waving makes my mouth go, "Mrs. Palmer! Mrs. Palmer!"

And it makes my brain go crazy all over the place.

I am thinking about all the Bible stories Mrs. Palmer has talked to us in this Sunday school room. All of the stories are bouncing around in my brain.

Like that story about that guy and his big fat fish and —

"Natalie?" Mrs. Palmer says. "Do you have a question?"

I have a hundred gazillion questions.

"Mrs. Palmer," I start, letting the first question come out loud, "can we do our play about that guy Moses getting SPIT out of that big fat whale fish? And how he got his daddy to give him a colored robe for Christmas?"

That girl Sasha says, "Mrs. Palmer, Moses didn't get spit out of the whale. That was Jonah." She says this without raising her hand.

Sasha turns a very not-smiley face to me.

"AND, it was Joseph who got a coat of many colors." She turns back around in her chair.

I give Sasha my best frowny face. Only she is already not looking at me.

We know about many Bible things and Bible people in this Sunday school class. I can't help it if they get mixed up inside my head.

Sasha is whispering to a boy who goes by the name of Peter. Peter is sometimes not very nice. Like Sasha. And he is this right now because he is laughing. And pointing at me.

This laughing and pointing makes my neck chokey. And my stomach twitchy in a not-nice way.

Jason waves his hand like crazy. He forgets the part about waiting for Mrs. Palmer.

"I want to act out Nat's play!" Jason yells. "I like that part about the whale spitting on Moses."

I really very like my friend who is a boy and goes by the name of Jason.

My bestest friend, Laurie, leans over and whispers to me, "I would like to act in your story too, Nat."

My neck stops being chokey. And my stomach isn't so twitchy.

I give my bestest friends smiley faces.

When I'm a famous movie-star actress, I'll always make movie-star parts for my bestest friend, Laurie, and also my bestest friend who is a boy, Jason.

And not Peter.

And not Sasha.

That's what.

Chapter 5

Pilots and Herod

"Thank you, Jason," Mrs. Palmer says. "Natalie's idea does sound interesting. But don't forget — this is a Christmas play, right? We want to do the Christmas story."

"I love that Christmas story!" I yell. Then I stick up my wavy hand because I forgot that part.

"Good," Mrs. Palmer says.

I try to remember all of the real live people in that Christmas story. Like Jesus and Mary and Joseph. Those guys are easy to remember.

Plus also, there are bad guys in that story. Like one bad-guy king with a hairy beard, who goes by the name of King Herod.

And another bad guy who goes by the name of Pilot.

Pilot!

I love those airy-planes! I rode one of those

35

things to go see Different Granny and Different Gramps. And that was really much fun until it got boring. And the guy who drove our plane went by the name of Pilot. Honest and for true! Pilot!

"Mrs. Palmer! Mrs. Palmer!" I yell. And I remember to use my wavy hand. "Can I be Pilot? Can I fly the plane?"

Sasha turns around and stares at me. Her eyes are little lines. Her mouth is a crooked sideways line. "Natalie, there weren't any planes when Jesus was born."

Sasha makes this liney face at me, like I am mixed up in my head.

Only I think Sasha is the one who is mixed up in *her* head and not me. On account of I know there was too a pilot in the Bible. And those pilots didn't fly camels or donkeys. They had to have planes.

"Were too!" I yell. "Don't you even know about that guy Pilot from the Bible?"

"His *name* was Pilate. *Not* the kind of pilot who flies a plane," Sasha says. Her voice is not so nice.

"They didn't even have cars in the olden days, Natalie. So they sure didn't have planes." Sasha sounds very much like a Smarty Pam or a Smarty Alex saying this.

Peter laughs his head off.

Sasha isn't even all done being Smarty Pam. "Pilate is in the Easter story," she says, like *she's* the Sunday school teacher. "King Herod is in the Christmas story. He talked to the wise men and — "

"That's enough, Sasha," Mrs. Palmer says.

I am glad Mrs. Palmer says this before Sasha gives away the whole entire Bible.

"There will be many parts in our play," Mrs. Palmer explains. "*Everyone* will get a part. And each part is just as important as the other parts."

"What parts?" Peter asks. He is raising his hand, but he didn't wait to be called.

Mrs. Palmer answers him anyway. "Well, we'll need an innkeeper. So we'll have the innkeeper's wife and son."

"There's not any innkeeper's wife and son in

the Bible, Mrs. Palmer," says Sasha the Smarty
Pam.

I think Mrs. Palmer gave up on that hand-
raising rule.

Mrs. Palmer says, "No, they aren't mentioned
in the Bible. Just the innkeeper. Still, he might have
had a wife and son, right? The Bible doesn't say.
Besides, this is a play, Sasha. We want lots of parts,
don't we?"

"Like what?" Peter yells.

"Of course," Mrs. Palmer says, "we'll need a
Joseph."

"You should be Joseph!" I yell over to my
friend Jason. I think Jason would be a very good
Joseph movie-star actor.

"You didn't raise your hand, Natalie," Mrs.
Palmer says. So I guess that hand-raising rule is
back.

"And we'll need a Mary," Mrs. Palmer goes on.
"Then Mary and Joseph will travel to Bethlehem.
So we'll need …"

But I'm not hearing this with my young ears. And that is on account of my brain is doing other stuff. Like it's making a picture of me riding a donkey and acting like I'm Mary. I very much like this picture my brain is making in my head.

I really, very much like this picture.

Plus also, riding that donkey is a hundred gazillion times better than flying an airy-plane. That's what.

Mrs. Palmer is still talking about how all of the parts in our Christmas play are so important and nobody should feel sad about getting a not-important job.

I try to get my ears to hear this.

I try to get my brain to hear this.

I try to get my stomach to hear this 'cause my stomach is very twitchy.

I try to get my heart to hear this.

And that is on account of this. I know honest and for true this true thing about me.

I want more than anything in the whole wide entire world to get that part of Mary in the Christmas play.

Chapter 6

Castles!

"Plus also, Mrs. Palmer said she would have to think about those movie-star acting parts in our Christmas play and not tell us who is what part until next Sunday school and Jason thinks that's on account of she knows she'll get everybody to come back next week only Sasha gave Jason a frowny face when he said that and she said *she* believed Mrs. Palmer would do the right thing in picking those parts plus she told Mrs. Palmer how pretty her hair looked today only it didn't so much look pretty and my bestest friend Laurie says she doesn't want one of those parts that have words to say with them and could she just be a not-talking sheep or maybe the inn."

I stop talking so I can breathe.

Nobody else in this car is talking.

Daddy drove so much fast that we are already

on my street.

"Plus also," I say after I breathe, "somebody gets to be Mary, Jesus' mommy, and I really, really, *really,* very much want that part of Mary who rides that donkey and gets Jesus!" Saying this loud is kinda scary. That's how much I want that part.

Mommy turns around and looks at my backseat. "Natalie, honey, every little girl in your Sunday school class wants the part of Mary. You can't all — "

"Not my bestest friend, Laurie!" I yell. Because I already said this in my regular voice, and Mommy's old ears didn't get it.

"Now, Nat," Mommy begins.

Only I can't wait for the ending. "I really *need* that part of Mary!" I say loud. "I *need* that Mary part more than any other Sunday school kid!" I think this is a true thing on account of I'm the only kid who is going to be a movie-star actress when she's grown up.

"I *have* to get the part of Mary!" My voice

squeaks up and down when I say this. Mommy will think this is whining. She hates whining.

But she doesn't say this 'cause Daddy turns Buddy very much fast into our driveway. Mommy has to hold on.

Daddy turns off Buddy and looks at my backseat. "Natalie, why don't you just be happy that you're going to be in a real Christmas play? I know you want to be Mary, but — "

"No, Daddy!" I say very loud. "I *need* to be Mary! If I can't be Mary, I don't want Christmas!" I fold my arms in front of my tummy. Like Mommy does when she's aggravated.

Daddy says, "Come on, Nat. Don't be so dramatic."

I know that word. And that is 'cause I'm going to be a movie-star actress. I think Daddy must not know that word on account of you're *supposed* to be dramatic in a play. That's what!

Mommy cooks up toasty-cheesy sammiches for lunch.

Daddy turns on TV and plops into his big chair that has a footstool on it when he leans backwards.

He always never watches cartoon-people shows, so I sit with Mommy and Percy in the kitchen.

"Man!" Daddy yells to himself and the TV. "What were they thinking? I can't believe that play!"

"Play?" I can't believe Daddy is watching a play. I run into the TV room.

But there's nothing on TV. Only boring football. Football is a stupidhead.

"Where's the play?" I ask.

"Huh?" Daddy answers. He isn't very good at talking and watching football together.

I watch giant guys in brown knock down giant guys in green. And you might could think that's fun to watch. But it's not.

I start to go back to my sammich. Only a commercial comes on. I love those things.

A cartoon doggie walks on just two legs and points at me outside the TV. "Christmas is almost here!" says the cartoon dog. "I have to get the perfect gift for my master."

Now the dog points to a little girl. "Lucky for me, I know what every little girl will want this Christmas."

I am listening very much. On account of I am a little girl this Christmas.

"A princess castle!" says the cartoon dog.

A big castle shows up and takes up the whole TV.

A little girl shows up and hugs the cartoon dog and hollers, "How did you know? A princess castle!

It's exactly what I wanted." Then she runs to that castle and goes inside. That's how big that thing is. She fits in there.

Plus also, that princess castle is purple. That's what!

I spin myself around to my daddy. "Daddy!" I holler. "I want that! Can I have that for Christmas?"

Daddy looks up from his toasty cheese. "What?" I don't think he even saw that purple castle.

"A princess castle! I want a princess castle for Christmas. It's purple, Daddy! And I can fit in there."

Mommy comes out where we are. "Honey, those castles cost a fortune."

"But I really, really *need* — !" I start.

"Besides," Daddy says, "where would we put it?"

"Everywhere!" I shout.

"We already have your Christmas present, Natalie," Mommy says.

"But I don't want that present. I want a princess castle!"

Daddy is peeking around me to see stupidhead football. He says, "Sounds to me like someone needs to go to her room and think about the true meaning of Christmas."

My daddy talks about "someone needing to go to her room and think" so much that I know the true meaning of "someone."

Me, that's what.

So I do this. I go to my room, and I think about that true meaning of Christmas. I know it's about Jesus and Jesus' birthday. And it's about God giving us his little boy, even though he only just had the one. And that's what that true meaning is about.

Only it also feels like it is about a princess castle.

Chapter 7

Waiting a Hundred Gazillion Days

The first thing I think of when I wake up the next morning is a princess castle. And this makes me smiley, thinking about that thing. I can see my bestest friend, Laurie, and me both fitting into my purple princess castle and playing princess.

But the next thing I think of is not getting that purple princess castle for Christmas. And that makes me frowny all over.

Then the next thing I think of is that Christmas play! I pop out of bed so much fast that my cat, Percy, pops out also.

"Percy!" I shout. "Guess what!"

Percy doesn't guess.

"I'm going to be Mary in a play about Christmas. That's what!" I say this to Percy on account of I want very much for it to be a true thing.

I run to the kitchen. Mommy and Daddy aren't doing anything except the newspaper.

"Mommy! Daddy!" I holler.

"Morning, Nat," Mommy says.

Daddy puts down the paper. "What's up, kiddo?"

"Me," I tell him. He is a slow waker-upper.

"Can we go to Sunday school?" I ask.

Daddy laughs and picks up his newspaper in front of his face.

Mommy is smiley faced. "Nat, it's only Monday."

"I don't care," I say.

"Sorry," Mommy says. "You'll have to wait until Sunday. How about some breakfast while you're waiting?"

I eat breakfast. But there's more waiting after that. And more waiting after that.

Mommy says my bestest friend, Laurie, can come over and play. And I didn't even have to whine to get her here.

There is some more waiting. Then finally, Laurie's big sister Sarah shows up at our door with my bestest friend.

"Hi, Natalie," Sarah says, very much like a grown-up, which she almost is. She looks down at Laurie, and her voice changes to not-so-much nice. "Don't get into trouble. Don't call my cell. Call Mother when you want to come home."

Sarah turns smiley faced to me again. "Bye, Natalie. Have fun."

"Bye," I say, watching her leave. Her long yellow hair isn't curly like Laurie's. But she is very much beautiful. Plus, she wears lipstick.

"What do you want to play, Nat?" Laurie asks when her big sister is gone.

If I don't come up with an idea, I'm afraid Laurie will. And that idea will be coloring. Coloring is boring and hard to do in between the lines.

The only idea in my head is that one I woke up thinking about. "I want to play in a princess castle," I say.

"Like *the* princess castle?" Laurie says. She gets very big in her eyes. "Oh, Nat! Did you get a princess castle?"

I shake my head in the no way. "But I very much want one of those things, and I told my mommy and daddy that I want one. Only they don't."

Laurie's eyes go back to regular. "Yeah. We pretty much get clothes and books at my house."

We go back to my room and sit on the floor. There is nothing to do in this room.

I make Mommy's air-going-out-of-a-balloon noise.

Laurie makes Mommy's balloon noise.

"Hey!" Laurie yells. "I know what we can play."

I wait because I know this will be a coloring idea. But I'm wrong.

"Let's play 'play'!" Laurie yells.

"Huh?" I ask. I don't get it. But it doesn't sound like coloring.

"Let's pretend we're putting on the Christmas play for the whole church to see," Laurie says.

I *love* this idea. I love it so much, I jump up off

the floor. "Can I be Mary?" I ask.

"You *have* to be Mary," Laurie says. "And I will be all of the people and animals that don't do talking."

"I have a donkey costume!" I yell. Because this is a true thing. I was a donkey on Halloween. "You can be the donkey."

Laurie makes a squealie noise. That's how excited she is to be a donkey.

I dig in my closet until I come out with my gray pajamas. Mommy sewed a tail on there. I keep digging, but I can't find that donkey mask.

"That's okay," Laurie says. She puts on my gray jammies right over her jeans. "We can pretend the donkey-head part."

"What about Mary?" I ask. "What should I wear for her?"

Laurie gets little in her eyes and her mouth, on account of that's how she does thinking. "In every picture I see of Mary, she has a scarf on her head. I think it has to be a white scarf."

"I don't have a white scarf," I say. I love my purple scarf. Only it has kitties on it. And that makes me have my next great idea. "Percy!"

My cat, Percy, is very white and fluffy and like a scarf Mary would wear. Plus also, he is sleeping on my bed.

"Do you think Percy will like being a scarf?" Laurie asks.

I pick Percy up and he hangs in my hands like a Mary scarf. "You can be in our play," I tell Percy.

I lift up Percy over my head and set him on my head like a Mary scarf.

Percy quits being saggy and hanging like a scarf. He is very much squirmy.

"Stop it!" I holler.

Only Percy doesn't stop it. He wiggles out from my hands. Then he jumps. He jumps very much hard.

"Ow!" I yell. On account of that jumping cat scratched my head. That's what.

"Are you okay?" asks Laurie.

"Percy is fired!" I say, touching my head where the hurt is. "Bad Percy. You can't never be Mary's scarf ever never!"

But Percy is already gone.

"It's not easy being Mary," Laurie says. "She had a very hard life."

I think this is a true thing.

Chapter 8

And the Answer Is ...

Every day I ask if we can go to Sunday school, on account of finding out about Mary in that Christmas play. And every day my mommy and daddy say, "Not yet, Natalie." Plus also, they say those words very much loud sometimes.

Every day I ask if I can have a princess castle for Christmas. On account of it still feels like I have to have this castle. And every day, my mommy and daddy say NO in different ways. Very many loud ways.

And that last NO way went like this.

"Mommy, could I *please* have a princess castle for Christmas? Please!" I ask hard.

We are at the dinner-eating table. And we aren't having anything good. Only just fish. And asparagus. So I have a lot of time to think about that princess castle. Plus also, I saw it on a commercial before dinner.

"Natalie, we've already been through this a dozen times," Mommy says.

This is a true thing. Only I didn't like the ending all of those times. "But I really *need* that castle!" I explain.

Mommy's eyes turn into line eyes. On account of she is getting aggravated. That's what.

Daddy stops chewing his fish. His eyes go to lines.

"Natalie," Mommy says, "you only want that castle because you saw it on TV."

"Did *you* see it on TV?" I ask. I'm thinking Mommy *should* see it like I did. Then she would want a princess castle too. And I would share.

"I saw it," Mommy says. "It's a fine castle. But you'll love what we got you too."

"And we're out of money now," Daddy says.

"That's not fair," I say. And it feels very not fair and kinda chokey. "I only just found out I need a castle. I couldn't tell you before."

Mommy makes her leaky balloon noise. "Nat, even if you'd asked earlier, we couldn't afford that thing. It costs as much as our refrigerator."

"I don't *need* a 'frigerator," I explain very much loud. My neck is all chokey. "I *need* a princess castle."

"Well," Daddy says, "you're not getting one. That's that. And I don't want to hear another word about it."

On one of those days, my bestest friend, Laurie, plus my bestest friend who is a boy, but not my boyfriend, Jason, both come over to my house. We play "play." Only not with Percy.

"I'm not being Joseph!" Jason shouts. Jason shouts really much. "Joseph doesn't get to ride the donkey. Anyway, I still want to do that other play, with Moses spitting at the whale." Jason spits into the wastebasket in case we don't get that part. "Let's go have a snowball fight!"

After a hundred gazillion more days, we go back to Sunday school. I am wearing my purple dress. I can't stop my mouth talking about the Christmas play the whole entire way to church.

At my class door, Daddy bends down and says, "Nat, just remember. There are no small parts. Only small actors." He kisses my head.

My daddy is not a movie-star actor. There are too small parts and giant big parts like Mary. Plus also, in my class, we are all small actors. That's what.

My bestest friend, Laurie, has a saved seat. And it is next to her. And it is for me. "Nat!" she yells.

I sit in that saved seat. My stomach is twitchy. My heart is thumpy.

Jason sits in the other next-to-me seat. His pants and shirt and hair are very much wet. And I'll bet he was in a snowball fight.

Mrs. Palmer walks to the front. She doesn't even have to tell us to quit being bumbly bees. "I know you're all eager to find out which part you'll play in our Christmas play," she says.

I sit up straight and try to look like Mary. I wish I had a white scarf that wasn't Percy.

"This is going to be such fun for everybody," Mrs. Palmer says. "We'll have almost two weeks of rehearsals."

"Mrs. Palmer! Mrs. Palmer!" I holler. "What's a 'hearsal?"

"A rehearsal is a practice," she answers. "We'll have play practices."

'Hearsal. I love that word. It is filled with fanciness.

We are starting to sound like bumbly bees.

"Shh-h-h!" Sasha yells.

I turn and look at Sasha. She is wearing a blue dress without fancies on it. And she has a big wood cross hanging on her neck. Plus also, she is wearing a scarf. But it's blue. Ha, ha.

"We'll start in the field with our shepherds and sheep," Mrs. Palmer says. "Rachel, Benjamin, and Travis are shepherds. Lisa and Dallas, sheep."

"Can you have a girl shepherd?" Rachel asks.

"What do sheep wear?" Lisa asks.

"Yes," Mrs. Palmer says at Rachel. "And I'll have costume instructions for your parents later."

She keeps giving parts out. "Katelyn, Seth, Brooks, you're the wise men."

"Wise MEN?" Katelyn hollers.

"We're just pretending, Katelyn," Mrs. Palmer says.

"That means we're three SMART men!" Seth yells.

"Yeah!" Brooks agrees.

Mrs. Palmer goes through the innkeeper, his wife and son, two other innkeepers. Plus almost everybody in that whole entire play. Except Joseph and Mary.

And so far, she hasn't made me anything. Or Laurie or Jason. Or Peter or Sasha. And my stomach is very many twitchy. That's what.

"Now, the part of Joseph," Mrs. Palmer says, "will be played by Peter."

"Yes!" Peter shouts.

"And the part of Mary ..."

Laurie grabs my hand and squeezes it.

I grab Laurie's hand and squeeze it back. I am hoping and wishing and —

"Goes to Sasha," Mrs. Palmer says.

My hand drops itself out of Laurie's. It feels like all of me drops with it.

"I'm sorry, Nat," Laurie says. Then she says something more. Mrs. Palmer says more somethings. But my neck is chokey and my ears are rumbly.

"So," Mrs. Palmer says, like it's all over. "Does

everyone know which part you'll be playing?"

I look at Laurie. All I know is what part I *won't* be playing.

Laurie whispers, "Trees. Jason and me and you, plus Bethany and some other kids. We're Christmas Bethlehem trees". She is smiley faced about being a no-talking tree.

Jason is shouting, "Me tree!" and jumping around.

My head feels muddy. My neck is more chokey.

I am not going to be Mary.

I am not going to ride a donkey.

I am not going to be a movie-star actress when I'm all grown up.

I am going to be a tree.

Chapter 9

'Hearsals

"Natalie, time to go!" Mommy yells. "You'll be late for rehearsal."

I throw my snow coat on the floor and stick my arms in and pull it over my head. This is how Granny taught me so my coat didn't end up backwards. "'Hearsals are stupidhead," I say. But my coat is over my head so only I hear myself say it.

Mommy drives me in the dark to church, even though it's snowing out here. And even though it isn't Sunday school day.

She walks me to Big Church. "Be good, Nat. I'll come back when it's over."

I want to go home with her.

"Nat!" Laurie shouts. She is standing with Jason and Bethany, being trees. Only Jason is also trying to scare the sheep.

My feet are draggy on the way there. Then I plop onto the floor of the stage. It turns out 'hearsals are when Peter and Sasha do things and talk words on the stage and the rest of us trees and sheep do not.

"Stand up tall, trees!" Mrs. Palmer shouts. "Natalie, did you ever see a tree sitting down?"

I stand up. But inside I'm sitting down.

Boring stuff happens.

I think it will be not so much boring if I run around like Jason. "Jason, you're it!" I say. And I tag him to make it a true thing.

I run.

Jason runs after me.

I run more.

"Natalie! Jason!" Mrs. Palmer shouts. "Stop! Did you ever see trees running? Bloom where you're planted. Let those roots go down deep!"

I hate 'hearsal.

After another day, we have another 'hearsal. And it's as boring as that other one.

"Mrs. Palmer," Sasha says in the middle of the 'hearsal, right when she and Joseph move into the barn. "Can we take a break, please?"

"Good idea," Mrs. Palmer says. "I need to get your costume handouts ready to send home with you. Some of your parents may have to get help making your costumes. I've tried to keep everything as easy as I can. Sheep, your costumes begin with white, woolly pajamas. You can sew on cotton balls. Trees, you start with pajamas and sew on what you need. Shepherds should be able to wear robes."

Sasha walks over to us sheep and trees. "My mother is making me a long Mary gown," Sasha says.

"Wow!" says Bethany the tree. "You're so lucky!" Bethany is a tree traitor.

"And I can keep wearing my costume when the play is over," Sasha says. "It can be like a princess gown. Only I'll get a crown instead of a scarf on my head."

"Wow!" says Bethany the Tree Traitor.

I try very hard to make Mommy's balloon-letting-out-air boring noise. Only I'm not so good as she is.

"And I'll need a princess gown," Sasha goes on, "because I'm getting a princess castle for Christmas."

"Wow!" Bethany says.

"You're getting a princess castle?" I say this

before I even know it. My heart is jumpy thumpy. My neck is chokey. "How do you know you're getting that thing? It costs as much as a 'frigerator."

Sasha wrinkles her nose at me, like she smells something yucky. "I know I'm getting a princess castle because I asked for one."

"All right!" Mrs. Palmer calls. "Break's over. Come and get your costume take-home papers."

Sasha is getting a purple princess castle for Christmas. My head says this to itself over and over.

"Here's your costume instructions," Laurie says. She hands me a sheet of paper with words and drawings.

My hand crumples up this paper all by itself. Then my legs start walking. And they don't stop until I am all the way in the back of church, where my mommy will come to get me.

I stand there and squeeze that paper very much hard. On account of doing this keeps tears from leaking out of me.

Then I throw that paper ball into the wastebasket.

Sasha, who gets to be Mary, is getting a princess castle.

And I'm not.

Chapter 10

Costumes

We have 'hearsals all week. They are still very boring.

"Natalie," Mommy says one night at dinner, "we better get to work on your costume. What did Mrs. Palmer tell you about the tree costumes?"

"I know," Daddy says, all smiley face. "The costume will *grow* on her." He laughs his head off. "Or, they'll just *leaf* it to us. Or maybe I'm *bark*-ing up the wrong tree."

"Very funny, Bill," Mommy says. Only she's not smiley faced like Daddy. "I don't know how to make a tree costume."

I am thinking that I don't even want to be in this play. That's what.

"Nat?" Mommy makes her line eyes at me. "Didn't your teacher say anything about your costume?"

I try to make my brain think. On account of it is already thinking my mommy is only a little away from being aggravated. I know I threw away that costume paper. But I remember. Kinda.

"Mrs. Palmer said we start with jammies and sew on leaves." I think this is a good job of remembering.

"What kind of leaves?" Mommy asks.

"Bible leaves?" I make my brain think again. In our Sunday school classroom, we have those Bible leaves hanging on our wall for one special Sunday when we get to wave those leafy things in Big Church.

"Really?" Mommy says. "You don't mean palm trees, do you?"

"That's it!" I say back. On account of we call that wavy Sunday "*Palm* Sunday."

Mommy wiggles her shoulders up and down. "Okay then. I'll use coat hangers. Or maybe wire. I'll get some green felt. We could ..."

She keeps talking. But it's mostly talking to her

own self about my play costume. Which is just fine with my own self. On account of I don't care.

More days go by. And more 'hearsals.

Mommy is making me try on my stupidhead brownish-greenish PJs with big green palm leaves sewed on there when the phone rings.

"I'll get it," Daddy shouts. Then he does. "Hello? Well, hi, Dad," Daddy says.

Only I know it's not his real dad 'cause his real dad is already in heaven, and they don't got phones in that place. This has to be Different Gramps and Different Granny. And they belong to my mommy. And to me too. Plus, they live a gazillion miles away in California.

"Fine. How are you?" Daddy is talking with one hand and waving at Mommy with the other hand.

Mommy goes over to the phone.

"Here's Kelly," Daddy tells the phone. "She wants to talk to you."

Mommy talks for a really much long time. And then it's my turn.

"Hi, Different Granny and Gramps!" I shout very much loud. On account of they have old ears. Plus also, they live a gazillion miles away.

"Hi, honey!" Different Granny says.

"Hey, Natalie," says Different Gramps.

They can say these things at the same time 'cause they got two phones going on.

"Ready for Christmas?" Different Gramps asks.

"Uh-huh," I answer. It's sometimes not so much easy to talk to a phone and pretend it's your different gramps.

"Did you get your Christmas tree all decorated?" asks Different Granny.

"Yep. Only you can't throw silvery stuff on there."

"Tinsel?" Different Granny says. "I love tinsel! Your mother used to love to throw it on *our* Christmas trees."

"She hates it now," I tell the phone.

We are kinda quiet.

Then Different Gramps asks, "So what are you getting for Christmas, Natalie?"

"NOT a princess castle," I tell them. "Sasha's getting a princess castle."

"Well, why aren't *you* getting one?" Gramps asks. "You tell that dad of yours that I said — "

"Now, Jim," Different Granny says. And it sounds very much like when my mommy says, "Now, Bill," to my daddy.

Gramps makes a grumbly sound.

"Sure wish we could be there to see you in your Christmas play," Different Granny says.

"I'm a tree," I tell her. On account of she won't feel very much bad missing me being a tree. "We have only one more 'hearsal to go, and it goes by the name of Dressed-up 'Hearsal 'cause we have to dress up for it."

"That sounds like fun, Natalie," says Different Granny. "Tell your mother to take pictures for us. We love you, honey."

"Merry Christmas, Natalie," Gramps says. "Send us some of that snow you're getting. Nothing but sunshine out here."

We say good-bye and wait for each other to hang up. Then I walk to the window and check on the snow. "There is very much snow out here!" I shout.

"Supposed to get a blizzard tonight," Daddy says.

In the morning there is more snow. It looks like a giant white swimming pool out there. My heart is very much thumpy.

Daddy is still in the kitchen and in his PJs. "Hey, Nat. Looks like we're snowbound."

Mommy comes over. "Natalie, Laurie's mother called. I'm afraid I've got some bad news."

I wait for the bad news. I already know I'm not getting a princess castle. Plus also, I'm not Mary. So I don't know what else could be bad news.

Mommy puts one hand on my shoulder. "Honey, they've had to cancel your dress rehearsal."

Chapter 11

Snowladies

"No 'hearsal?" I shout. This is a very much happy shout. On account of, in case you forgot, I hate those things.

"But the Christmas play will go on as scheduled," Mommy says.

My heart stops being thumpy.

"They should get our roads plowed by this afternoon," Daddy says. "But I called in to work. I'm taking the day off. I may just stay in my jammies all day. What do you think about that, Nat?"

I think this is a funny thing. It feels very much cozy in our kitchen with Mommy and Daddy still in their PJs.

"Can Laurie and Jason come over and play in the snow?" I ask.

"I doubt they could get their cars out," Daddy

says. Turns out that it's an okay thing. Mommy and Daddy and I stay in our jammies the whole entire morning. And that is very much fun, like it sounds.

After lunch, Daddy and I build a snowlady in our yard. Then Mommy brings out stuff for the snowlady's face. Like a carrot nose. And licorice sticks for line eyes. On account of our snowlady is aggravated 'cause it's so cold out here.

Later on, Mommy and Daddy sit on the floor under our Christmas tree with me and Percy. And we play Go Fish! Only not Percy.

Plus also, Old Maid. And I win. That's what.

We are back in our jammies for night, when there is a knock on our door. From outside of it.

"Knock, knock, knock!" shouts our door.

"Who could that be?" Daddy asks.

"Got me," Mommy says, heading for that knocking door. "Who would be crazy enough to drive on a night like this?"

She opens the door.

And that answer is ... my granny! That's what.

"Granny!" I yell. I run over and hug her. She is holding a big plastic box.

She hugs back. "Cold as a milk shake in Alaska out there!" she yells.

Daddy hurries up and takes off Granny's coat. "Mom, you shouldn't be driving in this."

"The day I let my son tell me when I can drive is the day I'll hop on that chariot to meet my Maker," Granny says.

Daddy hangs up Gran's coat. Mommy takes her

hat and scarf. But Granny won't let her take the big box.

"Would you like some hot chocolate? Tea maybe?" Mommy asks.

"Thank you, no," Granny answers. "In case you folks forgot, tomorrow is Christmas Eve. My granddaughter and I have cookies to decorate. She pulls up the lid on that big box, and there are cookies in there.

Granny makes Mommy and Daddy go to bed.

Then Granny and I go to our kitchen and pull out all kinds of stuff to make those white cookies fancy. Granny calls this a tradition.

We make lots of cookies fancy with red sprinklies and green frosting and silvery balls.

We are mostly talking cookie talk. Then Granny has us sit at the table. She hands us each a fancy cookie and bites hers.

"So, I hear you're not crazy about the Christmas play," she says.

I have been very smiley face doing these fancy

cookies. Now I don't feel smiley. "I wanted to be Mary."

"That kid, Sasha, gets to be Mary, right?" Granny says.

I nod and bite my cookie very much hard.

"Mary's a good part all right," Granny says. She licks the frosting off her cookie. "Of course, it's an easy part to play, being a human and all. Much more challenging to be something that's not human. Still, I think I'd rather be a tree."

I stare at my granny. She isn't laughing even a little.

"Why would you want to be a tree?" I ask her. I lick my frosting off of my cookie.

"God talks about trees all over the Bible, Nat," Granny says. "There was an important tree right there in the Garden of Eden with Adam and Eve. David and the other psalmists sang about trees showing God's power and grace. There were trees clapping their hands, dancing before the Lord Almighty!"

Granny sounds like a singer of Carol's songs just saying this.

"What else?" I ask.

"God says we're supposed to be like a tree planted by streams of water." Granny sticks that whole entire cookie inside her mouth. Her eyes close while she chews it up.

"Yessir," Granny says. "If I got to be in a Christmas play, I'd want to be a tree. The best tree I could be."

I fall asleep dreaming of snowladies and Mary and trees by water.

In the middle of the night, I wake up. Fast.

"Percy!" I shout. "I got to fix my costume." My granny made my brain think of this when she talked about trees and how God loves those trees.

Percy growls at me in a cat way.

I jump out of bed and turn on my room light and get my costume and my glue and my glittery. Then I put that gooey and glittery on my tree leafs.

I put it all over those leafy things. Until they are gorgeous.

When I'm all out of glittery, I hold up my new glittery costume to me. There is a streak of moon coming right inside my window. And I dance in that. I hold up my arms like tree branches waving over the water, and I dance.

When I climb back in bed, Percy curls up beside me.

"Percy," I whisper, "I'm gonna be the best tree I can be. Plus also, I am going to be the best tree *anybody* can be. That's what!"

Chapter 12

Really Much Christmas!

"Hurry!" I yell. "We'll be late!"

I'm already wearing my tree costume. I covered it up with my coat so it will be a surprise.

"You sure changed your tune about the Christmas play," Daddy says. He's putting on his coat and getting Mommy's for her.

"I love that tune," I say. On account of I love all those Christmas tunes and songs of Carol's.

Daddy drives to Granny's house and picks up Granny. She scooches into the back with me.

"How's my tree?" Granny asks. She snaps on her seat belt.

"I'm gonna be the best tree I can be!" I yell.

And I think this is a true thing. I want to be the best tree anybody can be. I want to be the best tree in the whole world. That's what.

In my head, I see pictures of everybody clapping for me. They are shouting, "More tree!" And Sasha is having to move out of the way so I can do my tree dance.

I am back to going to be a movie-star actress when I'm all grown up.

Mommy, Daddy, and Granny have to sit in the PUs.

I go back behind the stage. Loud bumbly-bee noise is coming out of there.

"Nat!" Laurie shouts.

"Laurie!" I shout. I run over to her and wiggle off my coat at the same time.

"Nat, we — !" Laurie stops shouting. Her mouth is still way open. She is very much big in her eyes.

Bethany stares at me too. She is also big in her eyes.

I stare back. And I see this. They are wearing very much different costumes. They are very much different trees than me. They are not palm trees at all.

I look around. Jason isn't a palm tree. So aren't two more kids.

Everybody but me is a Christmas tree.

"Look!" Sasha hollers. "Natalie's not a Christmas tree!"

Peter laughs mean. "Better make like a tree, Natalie ... and *leave!*"

Music starts, and Mrs. Palmer shoos us off the stage.

"I like your tree, Nat," Laurie says.

I want to say thank you, but my neck is too chokey. Those trees got mixed up in my head.

I want to go home.

Jason is running around chasing sheep. He zips past Laurie and me and stops. Stares.

I wait for him to laugh.

"Cool costume!" Jason shouts.

"See?" Laurie agrees.

I stop being chokey.

A very much long time happens. Sasha says words on the stage. Peter says words.

"Trees!" Mrs. Palmer whisper-shouts. "You're on!"

I hold my bestest friend Laurie's hand. Then we let go. On account of we are trees!

Plus also, I am back to being the best tree. That's what.

Mrs. Palmer gets a funny face when I walk past her, but she doesn't say anything.

I go to my tree spot beside the stable.

Sasha and Peter go inside to have a baby.

I sway my arms like a palm tree. I sway and sway.

There are Carol's songs going on in my head. Like "Joy to the World!" And like "Hark and Harold Angel Sing."

My feet start swaying. My swingy arms make me twist and turn. I twirl in a circle like a movie-star palm in the wind. Without roots. In the moonlight.

I prance across stage. I am a movie-star actor!

I dance across stage. A very famous movie-star actor!

I swirl past shepherds and sheep and wise kids.

I swirl into that stable.

I twirl and twirl and twirl all the way to that manger.

I stop twirling.

"What are you doing in here?" Sasha whispers mean.

I am staring. That's what.

I am staring at baby Jesus in that old manger. I

am looking very much hard at him. And I know it's just a baby Jesus doll. But it feels like something else. It feels like baby Jesus is right here for true. And that makes me shivery.

"Psst! Get out!" Sasha whispers.

Only I can't. On account of I can't stop staring at baby Jesus. He is very much little.

Peter says something. But my ears are buzzy. And it feels like he's far away. Like everybody's far away. Like nobody's here.

Except Jesus. And me.

There are tears leaking out of me. And I don't want to go anywhere but here. In this old stable. Not even if I had a princess castle.

And I think I don't even care about that castle. Or all the PU people watching. Or not being Mary. Or being a movie-star tree.

God let himself have this little bitty baby. In this old, stinky stable.

And I think I know something. I think this whole Christmas play isn't even about trees. Or

Sasha. Or even me.

It's about Jesus.

Nobody is doing talking out in the PUs.

I look up and see Mrs. Palmer beside me. But she isn't frowny at me for wrecking the play. She is smiley. Only with some tears mixed in.

I reach on my PJ leg and pull very much hard on one of my palm leafs until it comes off. Then I cover up baby Jesus in that manger.

I step backwards and pull off another leaf and set it on the floor of that stable.

And I keep on doing that. One big palm leaf and another one. And another. I'm backing up out of there. And when I'm out of leafs, there's a leafy road going to Jesus. And I very much like that.

Our whole stage and all the PU watchers are very many quiets.

I go all the way back off the stage. It's still really much quiet.

Then, like somebody planned it all along, we start singing. "Away in That Manger!" And the PU people sing too. We sing "Silent Night," and all of my favorite Carol's songs.

When we're out of singing, Mrs. Palmer calls all of us trees and sheeps and shepherds out on the stage with Mary and Joseph. All the PU people clap for us. And that feels like a good thing.

But not enough.

So I clap.

Then Jason claps. And Laurie. And the trees and sheep and Mrs. Palmer and even Peter and even Sasha.

Only I clap very much louder than anybody else. On account of I am clapping for Jesus.

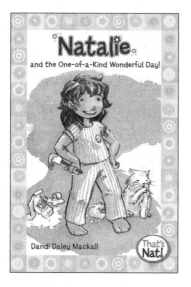 

Check out the other books in the series – available now!

Natalie has big five-year-old dreams for her future. So big, that her heart gets thumpy with excitement. Nat uses her very own words to tell about her hopes, struggles, and adventures. This makes the That's Nat! series perfect for young readers just ready for chapter books.

Book 1: Natalie and the One-of-a-Kind Wonderful Day!
ISBN: 9780310715665

Book 3: Natalie: School's First Day of Me
IBSN: 9780310715689

Book 4: Natalie and the Downside-Up Birthday
ISBN: 9780310715696

Book 5: Natalie and the Bestest Friend Race
ISBN: 9780310715702

Book 6: Natalie Wants a Puppy, That's What
IBSN: 9780310715719

My Little Purse Bible
ISBN: 9780310822660

This is an adorable purse-like Bible cover that comes with a complete New Testament edition of the NIrV translation with Psalms and Proverbs. This is available for a limited time and perfect for the Easter Holiday.

Available now at your local bookstore!

Adve
ISBN: §

Now ki
Bible f
writter
Kids!"),
to expl

The A
for E
ISBN: §

Buckle
Bible B
their liv
journe

Available n